Meg's Clothes

Written by Sally Odgers
Illustrated by Chantal Stewart

Meg has

a warm green coat.

nas

a warm blue scarf.

Meg has

warm purple boots.

Meg has

a warm orange hat.

5

Meg has

a warm blue scarf.

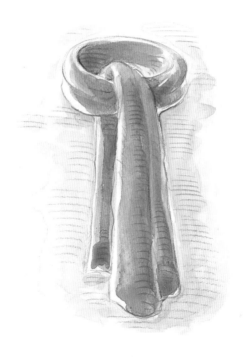

9

Meg has

warm yellow mittens.

11

Meg has

a **cold** red nose!